Norbert's Spooky Night

JAMES SUTHERLAND

Chapter 1

Dusk was drawing in around Finbar's field. It was the end of October and by six o'clock, the last slivers of sunlight were already disappearing below the western horizon. In the hedgerow, a blackbird (whose name was Geoffrey – 'Geoff' to his close friends) gave a final chirrup before turning in for the night; in his set, Jason the badger stretched his furry limbs with a yawn as he readied himself for a busy night's foraging for slugs, worms and other tasty treats. And underneath the big old sycamore tree, a horse stood, silhouetted in the deepening gloom, its head raised high as it peered anxiously up into the dark branches above.

"Colin?" Norbert called. "Are you there?"

A violent rustling high up in the leafy boughs confirmed that his best friend was indeed in residence that evening.

"Yes, Norbert, I am here," clucked an irritable voice. If you happen to have dipped into any of Norbert's earlier adventures, reader, you will already be aware that the 'Colin' in question was none other than Colin the cuckoo, Norbert's only friend. "And how might I be of assistance?"

The horse pawed the ground nervously with his enormous hooves. He knew that Colin didn't like to be disturbed in the evenings, but this wasn't just *any* old evening and there was something he urgently needed to ask his feathery friend.

"Erm…" he gibbered "I was just wondering what you were doing."

"If you *must* know, I was just finishing off the last chapter of this book I've been reading."

"Oh?" Norbert smiled. Colin was *always* reading books.

"Yes - it's a thing called *War and Peace* by some fellow named Tolstoy. Have you ever read much in the way of nineteenth-century Russian literature, Norbert?"

"No Colin."

"Just as I suspected. Well - I have to say it's rather good, if a little on the lengthy side. What was it you wanted, anyway?"

"I was wondering if it would be ok if I sleep underneath your tree tonight."

A strangled squawk issued from high in the treetop and seconds later, the cuckoo's beaky face appeared from among the leaves on a low branch, level with the horse's head.

"Certainly not!" he snorted, his eyes wild with horror. "We have had this discussion before, Norbert, and you may recall that we agreed that you would *never,*

ever sleep anywhere near my tree again on account of your *ridiculously* loud snoring."

"But..."

"I am afraid the matter is non-negotiable. I put it down to those gigantic nostrils of yours."

"But..."

"They produce a sound not unlike one of those Apache helicopters lifting off the deck of an aircraft carrier."

"But..."

"Even when you sleep at the furthest end of the field, I can still hear you."

"But..."

"I am sorry, my friend, but I must be firm - the answer is 'no'. Goodnight Norbert. Sleep tight. Don't let the bedbugs bite." And with these words, the grumpy old cuckoo turned to head back up through the leafy branches to his nest.

"But Colin," the poor horse whinnied in desperation "it's *Halloween*!"

There was another violent rustling from above and Colin's face reappeared.

"Halloween, eh?" he snapped.

"Yes."

"Norbert," the cuckoo sighed "you are a *horse*, for goodness' sake. Since when have you ever been worried about Halloween? Frankly, I'm surprised that you've even *heard* of it."

"But I *have* heard of it!" Norbert protested. "The sparrows in the hedge were talking about it this afternoon. They said it was a night when ghosts and ghouls and other scary things come out..."

"Goodness me! You should know better than to pay any attention to those chattering sparrows. *Ghosts? Garbage! Ghouls? Gobbledygook!* Why – I'm amazed that even a creature of your meagre intelligence would believe in all of that rot."

"But Colin, I'm *scared...*"

"Enough, Norbert. I can assure you that there are no such things as ghosts, nor are there witches, ghouls, zombies, spectres, vampires or any of the other supposedly 'scary things' that those pesky sparrows may have mentioned."

"But..."

"And even if there *were* such creatures, you can be certain that they would steer well clear of you on account of your terrible snoring. Now, if you would care to leave me in peace, I would like to finish my Tolstoy before it gets too dark. And so once again, Norbert, I must bid you goodnight."

"But..."

"*Bonne nuit* as they say in France."

"But..."

"Buenas noches amigo."

Chapter 2

A short distance away, at the bottom of the little lane that led up to his house, Norbert's owner, Farmer Finbar, stood back to admire the sign that he had just nailed to his gatepost. In a laboured, barely legible scrawl, it read as follows:

TRIK OR TREETERS KEEP OUT!

Although he had a vague suspicion that some of the spelling might not be *quite* correct, Finbar was nevertheless rather proud of his sign and was satisfied that it conveyed his intended message in the clearest possible terms. He had always *hated* Halloween – it was a night when groups of annoying children would tramp up the lane from the nearby village of Lower Bottomton in their silly costumes, expecting him to give them sweets or, worse still, *money!* This year, just in case any of the little blighters were foolhardy enough to ignore his sign, Finbar had taken the extra precaution of purchasing a small but powerful water pistol from the toy shop in the village which he intended to fire through the letterbox should he detect the merest hint of a knock at the door.

Convinced that he had taken care of the troublesome business of Halloween, he waddled back up the lane towards the farmhouse as fast as his chubby little legs would carry him. Finbar was no believer in ghosts and ghouls, yet there was something about the creak of the weathervane in the yard and the rustling of the wind in the trees that unnerved him a little, and it was with a considerable sense of relief that he locked the front door, kicked off his big, black wellingtons and sank into his favourite armchair with a hot cup of cocoa.

*

Down in the field, meanwhile, Norbert plodded unhappily to and fro, terrified at the prospect of spending Halloween night all alone. *If only Colin had let me sleep under his tree, I'd have been fine* he pondered miserably. *But wait – what was that?* Detecting a sound in the distance, he pricked up his ears. *Unless he was very much mistaken it was the sound of a car engine, and it was headed this way!* His heart skipping with excitement, Norbert trotted across to the hedge and peered over just in time to see a Land Rover pulling into the neighbouring field with a pink horse box in tow.

8

"Delilah!" he whinnied at the top of his voice, drawing a clearly audible 'tut' from the nearby sycamore tree. Delilah, for those of you unacquainted with the details of Norbert's love life, was the pretty pony who lived in the next field. Ever since he had first set eyes on her, Norbert had been head-over-hooves in love, though there had so far been little evidence to suggest that she felt the same way about him. More often than not, Delilah was away attending horse shows with her owner, a little girl named Jenny, but tonight, it seemed she had returned home in the nick of time.

From the other side of the hedge, Norbert watched with interest as a short, plump man hopped out of the driver's seat of the Land Rover and tramped round to the rear of the vehicle. The sight of Delilah emerging from her horse box was one which never failed to set the old horse's heart fluttering, as she had a habit of doing so with the grace and elegance of a model on a Parisian catwalk. This evening, however, it seemed that that she had no intention of turning in her usual performance.

"Come on, Delilah," Jenny's dad called. "Out you come." But from the horse box, there was no sign of movement.

"I said, come on!" he repeated with growing irritation. "I don't know what's wrong with you tonight, but if you won't come out, then I'll have to come in and get you…"

There followed and great deal of huffing and puffing as Jenny's father struggled with great difficulty to haul Delilah down the ramp.

"Careful Dad!" Jenny called from the Land Rover. "Mind you don't pull her reins too hard."

"Grrrr!"

Moments later, Dad clambered back into the car, his hair dishevelled and his face crimson with exertion. "Right," he grumbled "let's go before it starts to rain."

"Thanks Dad," Jenny beamed. "I wonder why she was so jumpy tonight, though. Maybe it's because it's Halloween…"

"Don't be so silly," Dad scoffed, turning the key in the ignition. "Horses don't know the first thing about Halloween!"

Norbert watched patiently as the Land Rover trundled away up the lane, the empty horse box clanking away behind it.

"Delilah?" he called as soon as the yellow glow of the headlights had faded into the distance. "Are you there?"

"Yes – I'm here," came the reply. "Hang on a second…" There followed a brief *clippety-clop* of dainty hooves, and the next thing he knew, Delilah had joined him on his side of the hedge.

But although he was delighted to see her, it quickly became evident that she was far from happy.

"Hello Delilah," he spoke warily. "Are you ok? You look a bit worried."

"Worried?" she snorted. "Of course I'm worried!"

"Oh?" Norbert frowned. "Why is that, then?"

"Because it's Halloween, you nitwit!"

"Oh."

"And I suppose you're going to tell me that you're not scared, are you?"

The question was a difficult one for Norbert to answer. *What could he say? If he told the truth and admitted that Halloween frightened him to death, she would think him a coward and all his long years spent trying to impress her would be in vain...*

"Of course not," he gulped, shuffling his hooves guiltily. "I'm not scared at all."

His words had an immediate effect on Delilah, brightening her mood in the blink of an eye.

"Oh Norbert," she beamed. "You're so brave! You'll think I'm being terribly silly, but would it be ok for me to stay in your field with you tonight? I wouldn't be scared

11

if I knew there was someone big and strong like you around."

"Of course you can," Norbert grinned as she pressed her warm body against his. "Halloween doesn't frighten me one bit!"

Chapter 3

Brrrrriiiiing!

The sudden sound of the doorbell had Finbar springing from his armchair like a gazelle. A slovenly, overweight gazelle, but a gazelle nonetheless.

"Garn!" he cried. "That'll be them pesky trick-or-treaters! Ignored my sign, did they? They'll wish they hadn't by the time I'm finished with 'em!"

His face flushed with fury, he seized his newly-purchased water pistol, hastily filled it up at the kitchen tap and crept through to the hallway. Stealth, he knew, was a critical factor in operations such as this; slowly, carefully, he opened the flap of the letterbox, poked the barrel of the water pistol through, and pulled the trigger.

The most rewarding thing, reader, about squirting ice-cold jets of water through letterboxes is the sound of the stricken cry of the victim on the other side of the door. It therefore came as a great disappointment to Finbar when, in the aftermath of unleashing his icy jet, no stricken cry was forthcoming. For several seconds he held his breath, listening intently, but on the other side of the door there was only silence.

"Strange," he muttered. Baffled and bewildered, still clutching the water pistol in his right hand, he rose stiffly from his combat position and opened the door to investigate.

*

Back in Norbert's field, the two horses stood quietly, side by side. As the sky had darkened, they had edged closer and closer together, their cheerful chatter dying away with the last glimmers of sunshine.

"Norbert?" Delilah whispered.

"Yes?"

"You know how I said I wouldn't be scared as long as I was with you?"

"Yes?"

"Well – I was wrong. I *am* still scared."

"Oh."

A short period of pensive silence followed as the two horses considered their situation. Norbert was the first to break it.

"Delilah?" he quivered.

"Yes Norbert?"

"I'm scared too."

Delilah turned to face him with a sigh. "I know you are," she whispered. "I can hear your teeth chattering."

In the little patch of woodland that bordered the field a twig snapped.

"What was that?" Delilah hissed, flicking her tail nervously.

"I think it was a twig snapping."

"I *know* that, you nitwit! What I meant was '*who* or *what* trod on the twig to make it snap?'"

Again the two horses again fell silent as they listened for any movement in the trees.

"Delilah?" Norbert whispered.

"Yes?"

"I'm *really* scared now."

"Me too! Come on – I think we'd better go and wake Colin."

*

There are times in all of our lives, reader, when we commit a foolish act which we instantly come to regret. In a life positively studded with blunders, Finbar had committed more than his fair share of foolish acts, yet there were none which he regretted more bitterly than his decision to blindly squirt water through his letterbox on that cold October evening.

He had, through the course of the previous year, been endeavouring to win the heart of a local lady who went by the name of Mrs Marjorie Maureen Muckleton. A widow who lived on a farm across the valley, Mrs Muckleton was a tall, boisterous woman whose face permanently bore the expression of an indignant gargoyle. In spite of this, Finbar had long loved her with a puppy-like devotion and had hopes of one day walking her down the aisle. Imagine his dismay therefore when, on opening his front door expecting to find a soggy trick-or-treater, he discovered instead a soggy and clearly unhappy Mrs Muckleton.

"Garn!" he gibbered as he studied her dripping form. Finbar was not an intelligent man but even he could see that, by dousing the object of his desire in freezing cold water, he had done little to help his romantic cause. If a gentleman wishes to charm a lady, he takes her out to dinner and showers her with expensive gifts; what he does *not* do is squirt her with ice-cold water. There followed what is sometimes referred to as a *pregnant* silence as they stood drinking each other in, neither able to give voice to the powerful emotions that gripped them in this most awkward of moments.

Sensing that an explanation of some kind might be in order, it was Finbar who spoke first.

"I'm ever so sorry about that, Mrs Muckleton," he gurgled, attempting to hide the water pistol behind his back "but I thought you were one of them pesky trick-or-treaters."

"Oh, you did, did you?" came the snarled reply. "And whatever gave you that ridiculous idea?"

Looking her up and down, Finbar was relieved to note that there was, in fact, something about her which he could use to get himself out of what was undoubtedly a sticky situation. "Well," he said gently "you are dressed up as a witch."

Though still seething with rage, Mrs Muckleton was forced to admit that the farmer had a valid point; she was indeed wearing a black, pointed hat on her head, with a long, black cape wrapped around her burly shoulders. She was not, however, what one would call a *forgiving* person and was certainly not going to allow a detail as trivial as the fact that she was clad in a Halloween costume to let Finbar off the hook.

"Are you seriously suggesting," she hissed "that my wearing a witch's costume gives you a licence to drench me in freezing cold water?"

"Oh no, Mrs Muckleton," Finbar replied hastily "of course not." And then, in a show of breathtaking bravery, he reached out and took her by the hand.

"I'll tell you what," he cooed "why don't you come inside and I'll put the kettle on while we get you dried off…"

Chapter 4

"Colin?" Norbert peered up through the dark branches of the old sycamore tree. "Are you there?"

"No, I'm not," came the reply from above.

For a moment, Norbert was confused. *If Colin wasn't there, how come he could hear his voice?*

"Colin?" he whinnied uncertainly. "You are there, aren't you?"

"No I'm not."

"Yes you are."

"No I'm not."

"Yes you are."

"No I'm not."

"Yes you are."

"No I'm not."

Sensing that little progress was being made, Delilah decided it was time to intervene.

"Colin?" she snapped. "This is Delilah speaking. If you don't get your fat, feathery, flea-bitten bottom down here right this minute I'll…" She paused mid-sentence as she detected the unmistakeable sound of a fat, feathery, flea-bitten bottom descending rapidly through the branches above her head.

*

"There you go, Mrs Muckleton," Finbar grovelled as he placed a steaming hot cup of tea on the table in front of his guest. "It's *luverly* to see you, though I must say it's most unexpected."

Mrs Muckleton fixed him with a look of contempt. "If you *must* know," she barked "I had come to invite you to a party."

"A party?"

"Yes – surely you know that the annual Lower Bottomton Halloween Party is being held down on the village green tonight?"

Her mention of the event touched a raw nerve in Finbar. He was indeed aware that tonight was the night of the party, however he had learned from reliable intelligence sources down in the village that Mrs Muckleton would be attending in the company of a certain Old Joe Baxter. A pig farmer who had recently moved to the area, Old Joe had also taken a shine to Mrs Muckleton and, in doing so, had instantly made himself Public Enemy Number 1 in Finbar's eyes.

"Oh yes," the farmer affirmed as he pulled up a chair beside her "I did know about it, only I 'eard you'd be going with that there Old Joe Baxter."

At the very mention of the name, Mrs Muckleton's eyes flashed with anger.

"Him?" she spat. *"Me? Go to the Halloween party with that low-life piece of filth? You must be joking!"*

"But Mrs Muckleton," Finbar gasped as a flicker of hope ignited in his heart "I thought you and Old Joe were an item…"

"After what he said about my witch's dress this evening? I think not, Mr Finbar."

"Dear me, Mrs Muckleton. What's the old so-and-so been saying now?"

"If you must know," she growled "we were just about ready to leave for the party when he had the impertinence to say that it made my bottom look big."

"Garn! Of all the cheek, Mrs Muckleton…"

"Exactly. Naturally, I informed him of my wish never to set eyes on him again for as long as I lived and sent him on his way."

"I'm not surprised, Mrs M…" The words died on his lips as Mrs Muckleton rose abruptly from her seat and turned around, affording him a grandstand view of her rear.

"*You* don't think this dress makes my bottom look big, do you?" she asked menacingly.

"Oh no, Ma'am," Finbar gibbered. "Not at all." In saying this, he was speaking the truth. The dress did not make her bottom look *big* – it made it look *GIGANTIC*, as though she was concealing an enormous sack of potatoes beneath the folds of black material.

"Good. I knew you'd see sense. Now – if you get your boots on, you can take me to the party instead."

Events were now moving much too quickly for Finbar's slow brain to process.

"B... But Mrs Muckleton," he stammered "I'd love to come with you but I can't – I don't have a costume, you see."

"Nonsense!" she snapped, looking him up and down. "I shall simply tell everybody that you've come as Frankenstein's monster. No one will know any difference."

"Garn!" Finbar exclaimed. Her words had wounded him deeply, and understandably so; no man likes to be told that he bears an close resemblance to Frankenstein's monster by the woman he hopes to one day walk down the aisle. But before he was able to protest, she continued in her usual brusque manner.

"Now hurry up, or all the sausages will have gone."

This simple statement had an electrifying effect on Finbar, animating him just as surely as the bolt of lightning had animated Frankenstein's monster. Where there had once sat a sorry and dejected figure, there was now a man on fire, a conqueror who would let nothing stand in his way.

"Sausages?" he drooled, leaping up from his chair. If you happen to have dipped your nose into any of Norbert's other adventures, reader, you will be fully aware of the strength of Finbar's feelings on the subject of sausages. If you have not, don't worry; you need only know that his love affair with the meaty snacks went far deeper than any other love affair that had gone before it. Romeo's passion for Juliet, Anthony's love of Cleopatra - these were mere shallow flirtations when set alongside Finbar's passion for sausages.

"Yes. Haven't you heard?" Mrs Muckleton continued. "Barry the butcher is providing the food for the party and he's using the opportunity to test out a delicious new recipe he's been working on."

"Garn!"

It was a widely accepted view among the citizens of Lower Bottomton that Barry the butcher's sausages were among the finest in the land. Finbar, however, went further than this; in his eyes, Barry was a Lord among men, a Demigod walking among mere mortals, and the news that he would be doing the catering at the party was therefore more than enough to dispel any lingering doubts in his mind.

"Right ho, Mrs Muckleton," he cried "I'll just grab my coat!"

Chapter 5

From his perch on a low branch of the sycamore tree Colin addressed the two horses in his sternest voice.

"Goodness me!" he scolded. "How many times do I have to tell you that Halloween night is nothing to be scared about?"

"But what about the ghosts?" Delilah shivered as a sudden gust of wind ruffled her mane.

"And the witches?" Norbert added.

"Not to mention the vampires," Delilah whispered.

"Ghosts? Witches? Vampires? Come on - surely even you, Norbert, aren't foolish enough to believe in all that rot."

"Yes, I am."

"I, on the other hand," Colin continued proudly, "am a man of science…"

"No you're not," Delilah cut in "you're a cuckoo."

"A trivial detail," the bird huffed. "But if it will keep you happy, I'll begin again. I am a *cuckoo* of science and, as such, am a firm believer that there is always a scientific explanation for any strange phenomenae we may encounter…"

"But we heard a twig snap in the trees over there."

"A twig?"

"Yes, Colin. It's a sort of small stick…"

"Norbert – believe it or not, I do know what a twig is. What I fail to understand is how, from hearing the sound of a twig snapping, you both appear to have arrived at the conclusion that the woods are crawling with ghosts, vampires and witches. Don't you see how utterly ridiculous this is?"

"Well – there was definitely *something* in there," Delilah hissed. "I heard it too."

By now, Colin was growing tired of the conversation.

"I'm sure you did," he scoffed "but has it not occurred to you that whatever it was that trod on the twig might have been something other than a ghost, witch or vampire?"

"But…"

"You don't think it could have been a badger, for instance? You know – those large, stripy, creatures that are known for rooting around in the dark? Or am I being silly?"

"But…"

"I happen to know for a fact that young Jason the badger is often snuffling about in those woods around this hour. I'm sure it must have been him that you heard." Satisfied that he had settled the debate once and for all, Colin flexed his wings in preparation for the short-haul flight back to up to his nest.

"No, Colin - it wasn't me," an urgent whisper came from somewhere down in the darkness in the vicinity of Norbert's hooves.

"Jason?" the cuckoo jumped at the sound of the voice. "Is that you?"

"Yes – I've been sitting here for ages."

"What the *earth* do you mean? I thought you'd have been out and about looking for insects and worms and whatever other foul garbage you badgers eat."

"No Colin. Not tonight."

"Why ever not?"

"Because it's Halloween and I'm scared."

At this, the cuckoo fluttered down furiously from his perch, landing with a muffled *PLOP* on top of Norbert's head.

"I don't know what the problem is with you three," he scolded. "I'm sure none of the other animals around here are bothered about Halloween."

"Yes we are!" a crowd of voices replied in unison.

As if on cue, the full moon emerged from behind a cloud, bathing Finbar's Field in its eerie light, and what the cuckoo saw there rendered him speechless; the patch of field beneath the sycamore tree was nothing less than a seething mass of wild animals of all shapes and sizes. Among the anxious crowd,

Colin counted three further badgers, eleven rabbits, four squirrels, seventeen field mice, a mangy-looking fox known as Brenda, seven sparrows, a wood pigeon with weight issues, three hedgehogs, two blackbirds and a weasel named Derek. *Clearly Norbert and Delilah were not the only animals feeling afraid that night…*

*

A short distance away, the annual Lower Bottomton Halloween party was in full swing. Gathered around a huge bonfire, all the village residents laughed and joked among themselves in their fancy dress costumes, eating and drinking to their hearts' content beneath the starry skies. All, that is, except for Finbar. Within minutes of his arrival at the party, things had hit a sour note when he had bumped into none other than his deadliest rival, Old Joe Baxter, whom he noticed was wearing a very expensive-looking vampire outfit.

"Finbar! What a nice surprise," he smirked. "But what's this – no fancy dress costume? Decided you were ugly enough without one did you?"

His words were cut short by a sharp *slap* across the face, courtesy of Mrs Muckleton. A solidly-built woman, blessed with the upper-body strength of a mountain gorilla, her blow was struck with sufficient force to send Old Joe's vampire fangs hurtling through the air to the other side of the village green.

"That was a wonderful shot, Mrs Muckleton," Finbar simpered as he watched his rival go stalking off to retrieve them. But when he turned around she had gone. Scanning the crowd, he soon spotted her loitering beside the tombola, chatting with an old friend of hers, Mrs Braithwaite, and so found himself at liberty to get down to the serious business of the evening; the locating of Barry the butcher's sausage stall.

*

"Will someone please explain to me what on earth is going on here?" Colin shouted, addressing the throng of animals standing in the pale moonlight.

A field mouse who went by the name of Miguel stepped forward bravely. "We've all come to spend the night under your tree where it's safe," he squeaked.

"Safe?" the cuckoo cried, aghast. "You don't mean to tell me that you *all* believe in ghosts and witches and all that other Halloween nonsense?"

"Yes, Colin – we do," the animals chimed in unison.

"Well – you can jolly well go off and be scared somewhere else! This is my tree and I won't be able to get a wink of sleep with you lot cluttering up the place. Now – if you don't mind…"

The words died on his lips – or rather, on his beak – for at that moment a spine chilling wail echoed through the night.

GAAAAAAAAAARN!

*

"Mr Finbar?" Barry the butcher leaned over the counter and peered down with concern at the figure writhing in the mud in front of his stall. "Are you ok?"

Finbar did not reply; no words could ever express the heartbreak he felt in that moment.

"There's no need to get so upset," Barry continued. "After all – it's only sausages…" He paused as the man on the ground let out another animal howl of despair.

The last time we saw Finbar, reader, you may recall that he had set out in search of Barry the butcher. This, he had duly done, drawn in like a bloodhound on the trail by the fragrant aroma of the maestro's sausages as they sizzled away on the griddle. On arrival at his destination, however, he was deeply dismayed to discover that a large queue had formed in front of the stall.

"Garn!" he grumbled as he reluctantly took his place in line to await his turn. Finally, after what seemed like an eternity, Finbar looked up to discover that he was next-but-one to be served. For a brief moment, joy burgeoned in his heart.

"Six hot dogs please, Barry," the man in front said, producing a ten-pound note from somewhere beneath his vampire's cloak.

"Garn!" Finbar cried. He recognized the voice as that which belonged to none other than his arch-enemy, Old Joe Baxter. The reedy, sneering tone was quite unmistakeable.

"Why hello there, Finbar," Baxter leered as he turned to walk away, his arms bulging with delicious hot dogs. "I hope you've got here in time – it looked as though Barry was running a bit low on sausages to me…"

Finbar did not reply; frantic and wild-eyed, he blundered forward to the counter and bellowed out his order. "Six hot dogs for me too, please Barry!" he screamed.

The butcher, however, was already untying his apron. "Sorry Finbar," he said shaking his head sympathetically "but I've done a roaring trade tonight and I'm all sold out. Old Joe there just had the last of the sausages."

"GAAAAAAARN!"

*

The animals in the field trembled with terror as the spine-chilling cry echoed all around the hills. It was unlike anything they had ever heard before, such was the anguish, pain and misery it contained. Little did they know that it was merely the sound that a greedy farmer makes when deprived of sausages.

"Colin?" Norbert whispered when the last echoes had died away. "Did you hear that?"

"Of *course* I heard it, you utter nincompoop!" the cuckoo hissed, the feathers on the top of his head standing up with fright. "I should imagine every creature within a hundred miles heard it."

"What do you think it was?"

"I have no idea. All I know is that it cannot have come from a human being, nor from any other creature I know of."

"Do you mean..." Delilah gasped, hardly daring to finish the question.

"I'm afraid so," the cuckoo spoke gravely. "A sound that terrible can only have come from a creature that is *not of this world.*"

"You mean like a ghost?" Norbert gulped.

"Quite possibly."

"Or a witch?" Miguel the mouse squeaked.

"Yes – I suppose it could just as easily have been a witch…"

"Or a vampire, perhaps?" quivered Derek the weasel.

"Yes," Delilah joined in "I think it might have been a vampire."

Colin had heard quite enough. "Look," he snapped "whatever creature made that sound, be it a ghost, a witch or a vampire, I, for one, have no desire meet up with it!"

"Then what can we do?" Delilah's voice wobbled as though she was on the verge of tears.

"One thing is for sure – we're not safe out here in the open," the cuckoo replied. "Come - you must all follow me. I know just the place where we can hide out until morning…"

Chapter 6

The full moon emerged from behind a cloud just in time to cast its light over the strange but orderly procession of animals as they crossed the yard at Finbar's Farm. Out in front was Norbert, plodding slowly along with Colin nestling on the top of his head, barking out instructions every few seconds. Behind him, Delilah trotted daintily, with the remaining creatures bringing up the rear. When they reached the barn, its black, ramshackle bulk looming over them in the darkness, the cuckoo ordered a halt.

"Miguel?" he hissed. "Are you there?"

"Yes," the mouse replied.

"Good. I just need you to sneak inside the barn and check if it's safe for us to go in."

"No thanks."

"I *beg* your pardon?"

"I said no thanks – I wasn't planning on sneaking into that barn at any point in the near future."

"Why not?"

"Don't want to."

At this, Colin fluttered from his perch down to where the tiny creature was standing and fixed him with one of his fiercest glares. "Now you listen here, young fellow," he clucked. "Do you mean to say that you are prepared to disobey a direct order?"

"Yes."

"Why – this is insubordination! What's wrong with the barn anyway?"

"There might be ghosts and witches and vampires and things in there."

"Poppycock! Of *course* there won't."

Miguel drew himself up to his full height (which was almost three inches) and looked the cuckoo in the eye defiantly. "What if there's an owl in there?" he demanded.

"An Owl? Owls don't live in barns…"

"I think you'll find that barn owls do, and they like nothing better than a tasty mouse for their supper."

"I guess you have a point," Colin sighed. "I suppose I'll have to find another volunteer…"

"Why don't *you* go?" Miguel challenged.

The cuckoo started violently. "I… Erm… I can't," he bleated. "It's simply out of the question, I'm afraid."

"And why is that?"

"Because if I go into the barn, who will be in command out here?"

"I don't mind taking charge," the mouse declared.

"Impossible!"

"Why not?"

"You're too short and hence lack the necessary authority."

"Napoleon was short."

"Yes, but he wasn't three inches tall, was he?"

"Mmmm" Miguel pondered, scratching his tiny chin. "If it's a question of size, then surely there's only one candidate for the job."

Realizing the implications of the mouse's words, Colin shuddered from head to toe. "S… Surely you're not suggesting…"

"Absolutely – I'm sure Norbert would make a fine leader."

"Norbert?" Colin squawked *"Are you stark-raving mad?"*

"Not particularly."

"Norbert couldn't *possibly* take charge – he has a brain the size of an amoeba, haven't you, Norbert?"

"Yes Colin," the horse agreed.

At that moment, an owl hooted in a nearby tree. Carried by the wind, it took on a strange and spooky quality; suddenly the idea of going inside the barn didn't seem like such a bad one after all.

"Very well," Colin volunteered hastily. "I shall go in. Norbert – I am placing you in command of operations out here. May the Lord protect you all!" And with these fateful words he squeezed his plump, feathery form

through a crack in the barn door and
disappeared into the darkness within.

*

"Finbar! Stop this nonsense at once!"
Mrs Muckleton barked at the fat farmer as
he writhed on the muddy ground at her feet.

"But Mrs Muckleton," the farmer sobbed
"you don't understand… The hotdogs are
g… g… *gone!"*

"Gone?" she sniffed. "What on earth are
you talking about?"

Filthy dirty and wild-eyed, Finbar hauled
himself to his feet and addressed her in a
hoarse, strangled voice. "It was that Old Joe
Baxter, Mrs Muckleton – he's had 'em all
before I could get to the front of the queue!"

The village of Lower Bottomton was
quite unaccustomed to such high drama, and
Finbar's cries had drawn a large crowd,
much to Mrs Muckleton's growing
embarrassment.

"For goodness' sake!" she hissed. "Can't
you just eat something else?"

"Something else?" the farmer staggered
back in horror at the suggestion. *Did she not
understand that, apart from sausages, there
<u>was</u> nothing else in life?*

"Yes – I'm sure there are veggie burgers
left."

36

This was too much for Finbar; turning on his heels, he let out a further strangled cry of despair and fled into the watching crowd. Seizing his opportunity, a tall, rakish figure clad in a vampire costume stepped forward.

"Good evening, Ma'am," Old Joe Baxter smirked. "I'm sorry to see that Finbar's making a fool of himself again."

Still furious about his earlier remarks concerning the size of her bottom, Mrs Muckleton eyed him with cold distain. "He has done nothing of the sort," she replied stiffly. "From what I can gather, Mr Finbar is most upset that you purchased the last remaining hot dogs from Barry the butcher."

"That's a shame... A *terrible* shame," Baxter sniggered. "The thing is, though, Mrs Muckleton – I didn't buy all those hot dogs for myself..."

"Oh?"

"No – I made sure I bought plenty just in case you wanted one." With this, he reached into his vampire's cape and produced a fat, juicy hot dog nestling in a floury bun and handed it to her.

In the watching crowd there was a disturbance; Mrs Muckleton turned just in time to see Finbar's burly form blundering towards her, his bloodshot eyes fixed on the treasure that she held in her palm.

"Right!" she exclaimed. "I've just about had enough of this! Why - I've never been so embarrassed in all my life!"

And with these words, before anyone had the chance to stop her, Mrs Muckleton turned, took careful aim, and hurled the precious hot dog high above the watching crowd and into the bonfire.

"GAAAAAAARN!" came a heart-rending cry from the near vicinity.

Chapter 7

"Is there anyone there?" Colin hissed, his heart beating hard in his feathery chest. Inside the barn it was so dark that he could barely even make out the end of his own beak. He was about to slip back outside to inform the others that the coast was clear when, from somewhere in the darkness, a small, high-pitched voice replied.

"Yes," it said "we are here."

*

It was a foul-tempered Old Joe Baxter that stalked away from the annual Lower Bottomton Halloween Party. He had been *sure* that his generous offer of the last remaining hot dog would be sufficient to melt Mrs Muckleton's heart and it had therefore come as a nasty shock when she had taken this, his token of love, and heaved it into the bonfire. Old Joe was not, generally speaking, a sensitive man, but her actions had hurt him deeply. The thing, however, that irked him most of all was that, in spite of everything that had occured, she had chosen to stay at the party with Finbar!

"What she sees in the fat old fool, I'll never know," he muttered. "Still – the night

ll teach 'em to mess with
r…"
these words, he left the main
aded up the hill towards Finbar's
wicked eyes glinting in the
ht.

*

"Who goes there?" Colin quivered,
squinting up through the blackness of the
barn towards the mysterious voices. "I am
warning you – I am fully trained in the art of
ju-jitsu."

"Fear not," the voices replied in unison
"we mean you no harm."

"Really?" the cuckoo almost sobbed with
relief. "Well – if you're quite sure about
that, perhaps you'd better come down here
where I can see you."

"Very well." A light, barely audible
fluttering sound came from high up in the
rafters, followed by a series of tiny *plops* as
a host of small creatures landed in the straw
around Colin's feet.

"I say," he clucked "be careful – you
nearly landed on my head!"

"We're sorry," one of the creatures
squeaked. "Please don't be angry with us."

"Very well. I suppose I'll forgive you this
once, so long as you understand that I can

40

only be pushed so far." Colin now spoke with growing confidence. Although he was significantly outnumbered by the creatures, his eyes had adjusted to the dark enough to see that they were tiny, fragile little things who were clearly more frightened of him than he was of them. "What sort of fellows are you anyway?"

"We are bats. This barn is our home. My name is Barry. These are my brothers Bobby, Bertie and Benny, and over there is my sister, Barbara, my cousin Beryl and my mother, Belinda. Just behind her is my cousin Barney and..."

"Fascinated though I am by the details of your family tree," Colin cut in impatiently, "I would be even more interested to know why you're not out and about tonight catching moths and insects and whatever other garbage you bats like to eat."

"You must be joking! We wouldn't go out tonight for all the tea in china."

"Why not?"

"We're too scared – it's Halloween, you know!"

"Are you serious?" the cuckoo gasped. "Bats scared of Halloween? I'd have thought it would be the best night of the year for you lot!"

"I'm afraid not," squeaked Barry.

Then an idea struck Colin. "Well," he said "if you are indeed frightened, it may interest you to learn that I have a whole platoon of animals waiting outside the door."

"Oh?"

"Yes – they are all highly trained and capable of repelling even the most determined attacks from vampires, witches and ghosts. If you like, I could ask them to come in and spend the night here."

"Could you really?" Barry's little voice was almost bursting with gratitude. "Wow! That would be so kind of you…"

"Think nothing of it. Kindness is my middle name. Norbert?" he called, poking his head out through the barn door.

"Yes Colin?"

"Are you still out there?"

"Yes Colin."

"Then feel free to join me in here. Just mind you don't tread on any bats with those clomping great hooves of yours."

*

Old Joe Baxter cut a sinister figure as he crept into Finbar's yard, the bright moonlight casting long shadows of his lanky figure across the ground. As he was still wearing his vampire costume, it had occurred to him that the very least he could do to get his revenge on Finbar would be to give him a nasty fright when he returned home that night. The plan he had formulated was a simple one; he would conceal himself behind the coal bunker next to the front door of the farmhouse and lie in wait for the farmer's return, upon which, he would spring from his hiding place in his vampire outfit and scare the old fool out of his wits. Rubbing his hands with glee, Old Joe slinked over to the bunker and took up his position.

Five minutes passed, then another five. By the time fifteen minutes had elapsed, he began to wonder whether his plan was quite as cunning as he had first thought. *Had he simply headed home,* he pondered, *he would now be sitting toasting his feet in front of a log fire with a cup of hot cocoa; instead, he was squatting in a place that was cold, damp and dirty. And unless he was very much mistaken, a spider had just crawled down the back of his neck and was now heading due-south down his spine towards his underpants. Still* he thought, *it'll all be worthwhile when I scare the socks off old Finbar…* His resolve stiffened, Baxter resumed his squatting behind the coal bunker. Seconds later it began to rain.

"Drat!" he cursed under his breath as the first heavy drops pitter-pattered on his vampire's cloak. But he had already suffered too much to simply give up and head home. Poking his head above the coal bunker, he scanned the terrain in search of shelter. *Wait... What was that over there? A barn! And the door was ajar!* Without further ado, Old Joe emerged from behind the bunker, tip-toed across the moonlit farmyard on his spindly legs and slipped inside...

Chapter 8

Down at the Lower Bottomton Halloween party, things were beginning to draw to a close. Many of the guests had already left and were streaming home through the village in their fancy dress costumes. Huddled beside the dying embers of the bonfire, Finbar and Mrs Muckleton stood side by side, their faces glowing red in the firelight. Had it been any other couple, the scene would have been quite romantic; romance, however, was not an emotion with which Mrs Muckleton was familiar.

"Well Mr Finbar," she yawned "I think I've had enough for tonight. I'm going home."

"Home?" the farmer gasped with dismay. He had been under the impression that Mrs Muckleton was finally warming to his advances, and he had no intention of letting her slip from his grasp so easily. Then an idea struck him…

"It's just that I was 'oping you might like to come back to my 'ouse for a coffee," he grovelled, trying without success to drape his arm around her massive shoulders.

"A coffee?"

"Yes Mrs Muckleton."

"At your house?"

"Yes Mrs Muckleton."

Folding her brawny arms, she glowered down at the chubby farmer. Beneath her hard exterior she had one weakness, which was that she believed strongly in the supernatural. In her mind, ghosts, witches, and vampires truly existed and she had not been relishing the prospect of walking home alone along the dark country lanes.

"If I agree to come back to your house for a coffee, will you promise to escort me home afterwards?" she growled.

"Oh yes Mrs Muckleton!" Finbar beamed, almost hopping up and down on the spot with delight. "Of *course* I will."

"Very well then – you may lead the way…"

"Right ho, Mrs Muckleton!"

"As long as you understand that my coming to your house for a coffee does not mean that we are an item, nor that I am necessarily fond of you in any way."

"Garn!"

*

In the gloom of the barn, the animals gathered silently. Some, including the horses, stood, whilst others lay down in the hay or cuddled up against each other for warmth as the wind whistled through the cracks in the rickety walls.

"Is it morning yet, Colin?" Norbert whispered through the darkness.

"For goodness' sake Norbert," came the hissed reply "that's the third time you've asked me that in the past five minutes!"

"Oh?"

"I've told you – it's just about to turn midnight and…" The cuckoo froze mid-sentence as the barn door opened with a loud creak and a tall, shadowy figure stepped inside.

When Old Joe Baxter had entered the barn to seek shelter from the rain, he had done so in the belief that it would be empty; what he had not anticipated was that it would be utterly packed to the rafters with animals of all shapes and sizes. It therefore came as a great surprise to him when he stepped on something soft and subsequently received a powerful bite to his left ankle. An easy-going sort, Jason the badger was, like Ghandi, a firm believer in non-violence. Even the staunchest pacifists, however, tend to draw the line at being trampled all over by size-nine boots, and in doing this Old Joe Baxter had simply pushed Jason too far…

"Aaaaaaargh!" the unfortunate man roared as he took a frantic sideways leap in the darkness. Tragically for him, this leap

conveyed the size-nine boots directly onto the outstretched, bushy tail of Brenda the fox. Following Jason's example, she did not hesitate to sink her teeth into Old Joe's other ankle.

"Aaaaaaaaaargh!" Baxter roared again, even louder than before as he sprang in a north-westerly direction only to receive a nasty bite on the shin courtesy of Derek the weasel. For several minutes the painful scene continued, with Old Joe leaping back and forth in a kind of crazed Irish jig as he frantically sought a means of escape. It was only after he had been bitten for the seventeenth time that his misery was brought to a merciful end, when a powerful kick from Delilah sent him hurtling out through the barn door and back out into the farmyard, where he finally came to rest in a heap of manure. His eyes wild with terror, Old Joe Baxter picked himself up and fled off down the lane as fast as his lanky legs would carry him.

*

Inside the barn, chaos reigned; convinced that they were under attack from a vampire, the animals had worked themselves up into a stampede and were in grave danger of injuring one another.

48

"Please!" Colin cried, fluttering his way up to the safety of a low rafter. "Everybody calm down!"

One by one, realizing that their attacker was no longer among them, the animals ceased their stampeding and calmed down as requested. Within a matter of moments, the barn was still once again.

Norbert, who had simply waddled to and fro in vague bewilderment throughout the whole episode, was the first to speak.

"Colin?" he said. "What happened just then?"

"In all honesty, Norbert – I'm not really sure. All I know is that we came under attack, although from what I cannot say."

"I saw it," Miguel the mouse piped up from somewhere down among the straw "it was a vampire."

"A vampire?" Colin scoffed. "Come now - everyone knows that there are no such things as vampires…"

Miguel, however, was sticking to his guns. "Mice can see better in the dark than cuckoos," he squeaked "and I'm telling you that it was a vampire!"

"I saw it too," Jason the badger affirmed. "It trod on my foot as a matter of fact."

Colin listened with growing alarm as, one after another, all of the animals able to see in the dark testified that they had seen the vampire.

"I see," he gulped when they had finished. "Well, my friends - you know what this means, don't you?"

"No," Norbert replied simply.

"It means we're not safe here, you big nincompoop! For all we know, that vampire might reappear at any moment with reinforcements?"

Norbert shifted on his hooves uneasily as he considered the situation. "But Colin," he whinnied "there's nowhere else for us to go."

"There is *one* place left where we can hide," the cuckoo declared in a strangely nervous voice. "Come on, everybody – follow me!"

Chapter 9

"Please Mrs Muckleton," Finbar wheezed as they marched side by side along the moonlit hedgerows, "will you slow down a bit." For each of her long strides, he was forced to take at least three waddling steps on his short little legs.

"I *do* wish you would keep up," she replied crossly, quickening the pace even more. "It's very late and I'm getting cold." It was only when they turned off the main road onto the little lane which led up to Finbar's house that she came to a sudden halt.

"Listen!" she hissed.

Finbar listened. "I don't 'ear anything," he hissed back.

"Shhh!" Mrs Muckleton pressed a finger to her lips. "There… Do you hear it now?"

The farmer strained his ears, struggling to detect anything over the sound of his own heavy breathing. *Then he heard it; the sound of footsteps… Somebody was running down the lane, heading directly towards them…*

"Garn!" he whispered.

The word had barely left his lips when the unmistakeable figure of Old Joe Baxter came haring round the bend in the lane, moving like a greyhound on a racetrack. So intent was he on fleeing for his life that he completely failed to notice Finbar and Mrs Muckleton until a loud bellow from the latter brought him to a sudden halt.

"Joe Baxter!" she barked. "What on earth do you think you are doing, jogging at this time of night?"

"Jogging?" Old Joe gasped, his eyes wild with terror. "Oh no, Mrs Muckleton - I wasn't jogging. You see…"

"Just look at the state you," she continued, running her eyes up and down his dishevelled figure. "Goodness me – whatever has happened to your trousers?"

Half dazed, Old Joe peered down at his legs and noticed for the first time that the trousers of his vampire costume were hanging in shreds, a testament to the ferocity of the attack by the animals in the barn. Curious to examine his rival's leg-wear for himself, Finbar chose this moment to step out from behind Mrs Muckleton's gigantic shadow.

"Hello there, Joe," he grinned. At the very sight of him, Baxter quivered from head to toe.

"Finbar!" he wailed, backing away in terror. "This is all *his* fault, Mrs Muckleton! The man is insane!"

Mrs Muckleton was confused. "Heavens above, Mr Baxter," she exclaimed. "Are you seriously accusing Mr Finbar of tearing at your trousers? I've been with him all night and am quite certain that he has done no such thing."

"No, Ma'am, it's just that…"

But Mrs Muckleton had heard quite enough.

"Come on, Mr Finbar," she interrupted "let's leave this lunatic here and get that cup of coffee you promised me."

Her words drew a sharp cry from Old Joe. "*Please* Mrs Muckleton, you can't go up there with him!"

"Mr Baxter – for the last time, I shall go wherever I want to..."

"But it's not safe! *Finbar's* the lunatic, not me! He keeps wild animals in his barn!"

Now it was Mrs Muckleton's turn to quiver violently. "Is this true?" she glowered, turning to the farmer. "Do you keep wild animals in your barn? You know I don't like animals…"

"Of *course* I don't!" Finbar snorted. "If you ask me, Old Joe there's gone off his rocker."

"But please," Baxter wailed. "You *have* to believe me…"

"Believe you?" Mrs Muckleton snarled, swatting him aside. "I've never heard such nonsense in all my life. Come on, Mr Finbar – let's go!"

*

In their new hideout, the animals huddled together once again, each hoping they would get through the remainder of the night without further incident.

"Colin?"

"Yes Norbert?"

"Is it nearly morning?"

"No Norbert."

"Oh."

There followed a lengthy silence.

"Colin?"

"Yes Norbert?"

"Are you *sure* we're safe here?"

"Yes - for the umpteenth time, we are *perfectly safe!* Now go to sleep – you're keeping everyone awake with your pointless chit-chat."

"Ok Colin."

Satisfied that all was well, the big old horse gave a contented yawn, closed his eyes and was soon sound asleep.

*

"Here we are, Mrs Muckleton," Finbar simpered as he opened the farmhouse door and switched on the light in the hallway. "You can hang your witch's hat and cloak on the peg there if you like."

"No thank you, Mr Finbar. It's freezing in here, so I shall be keeping them on."

"Very good, Mrs Muckleton. How about if you go through to the sitting room and make yourself comfortable – the door's just there on the right - while I head on through to the kitchen and make you a *luverly* cup of coffee."

"Very well," she replied. "Milk and two sugars please, and don't be long!"

Having watched him disappear off through to the kitchen to make the coffee, Mrs Muckleton paused in front of an old, cracked mirror that hung in the hallway to study her reflection. As she did so, she experienced a most peculiar sensation unlike anything she had ever encountered before; it was a feeling of mild affection towards Finbar.

True, he was a little overweight, if not downright podgy. Nor could it be denied that he was a first class fool with the mental capacity of a prawn sandwich. And yet in spite of these things, he did possess some of the qualities one would wish for in an ideal husband; he was loyal and obedient, he had his own house, and most importantly of all he was, unlike Old Joe Baxter, essentially sane.

Satisfied that she was looking *even* more beautiful than ever, Mrs Muckleton turned and made her way across to the sitting room door and reached for the handle…

Chapter 10

"Well, Finbar," the farmer muttered to himself as he flicked on the kettle "it's a funny old world. There I was this very morning, thinking how much I hated Halloween, and then it turns out to be the thing wot's finally brought me and Mrs Muckleton together! And as for that Old Joe Baxter – I doubt we'll be seeing anything more of him for a very long time. I wonder what he was doing running down the lane at that time of night. I wouldn't be surprised if…" He broke off mid-sentence as a blood-curdling scream issued from the hallway.

"Garn!" he cried, the coffee cup tumbling from his trembling hand, smashing into pieces on the hard stone floor. "Don't worry, Mrs Muckleton – I'm coming!"

*

Mrs Muckleton did not let loose her scream immediately on opening the sitting room door. She was, after all, a hard woman with nerves of steel and muscles like iron bands. No, reader; the most accurate way to describe her reaction on opening the door would be to say that she *goggled.* And then she goggled some more. She may even have *gawped,* though there were no reliable witnesses to confirm this. And the reason, reader, for all this goggling and gawping was that, unless she very much mistaken, Finbar appeared to have transformed his living room into a sort of wildlife park, containing every species of creature native to the British Isles. Her jaw hanging open with disbelief, she stood for a moment in silence as she scanned the room from left to right, drinking in the extraordinary scene. Amidst the teeming horde, she spotted weasels, foxes, badgers, horses, rabbits, hedgehogs, ducks, mice, squirrels and even a cuckoo - a fat, mangy cuckoo, to be more precise – all sound asleep.

Mrs Muckleton took a deep breath. *Old Joe had been right all along; Finbar was indeed a madman! All she needed to do, she told herself was to remain calm and humour him until the opportunity to escape presented itself. Once she was safely back in her own home, she would call the relevant authorities and have him taken away to a suitable institution where he could be cared for appropriately and would no longer represent a danger to the public...*

Slowly, carefully, she took a step backwards towards the safety of the hall and would doubtlessly have escaped undetected had the sharp point on her witch's hat not prodded a sleeping bat, hanging upside down from the doorframe above her head. Barry the bat (for it was he that she had prodded) took great exception to being awoken thus; with a loud squeak of indignation, he took to the air and proceeded to whirl around the living room like an angry wasp. For Mrs Muckleton, who had a terrible phobia of bats, this was the final straw, and it was now that she opted to let forth with her blood-curdling scream.

"Bleeeeeeeeeurgh!" she wailed. Turning on her heels, she charged out into the hallway, screaming at the top of her voice, only to collide heavily with Finbar as he emerged from the kitchen.

"Oof!" the farmer groaned as he hit the floor with a *BANG!* Dazed and bewildered, he raised his head from the floorboards just in time to see his beloved disappearing out through the front door.

"Wait!" he cried. "What about your coffee?"

But Mrs Muckleton was by now in full flight. It is possible that, were he present, Usain Bolt *might* have kept pace with her as she sped off down the lane, though even he would undoubtedly have struggled. Finbar, certainly, stood no chance; the most he could manage was a few waddling steps down the driveway before he sank to his knees with an exhausted Garn!

*

Back in the sitting room, there was pandemonium as frightened animals, awoken suddenly by Mrs Muckleton's scream, dashed to and fro, upturning furniture and causing general mayhem.

From his vantage point on the mantelpiece, Colin took a deep breath and addressed the surging crowd in his sternest voice.

"Order!" he squawked. "Everybody calm down!"

He spoke with the kind of commanding authority one would expect from a cuckoo of his seniority, and within a matter of seconds the room was still.

"Now then," he said "did anybody see what it was that made that noise?"

"I did," squeaked Barry the bat "it was a witch!"

"A witch?" the cuckoo gasped. "Are you quite certain?"

"I saw it too." Derek the weasel confirmed. "She had the most *hideous* face and was wearing a big pointy hat."

"Goodness me!" Colin quivered. "First we are attacked by a vampire, then we are assailed by a witch – it would seem that nowhere is safe tonight…" A murmur of anguish went up among the listening crowd. "Unless..."

"Unless what?" Delilah urged.

"Unless we stay right where we are, in this farmhouse," Colin continued "only *this* time, each and every one of us must find a place to hide…"

There followed a frenzy of activity as animals charged back and forth seeking out nooks and crannies in which to conceal themselves. Badgers ducked behind sofas, ducks ducked behind badgers. Hedgehogs hid in chests of drawers and in the kitchen, rabbits and squirrels took refuge in the cupboards, whilst mice squeezed in behind the fridge. Even Brenda the fox managed to find a suitable hidey-hole in the closet underneath the stairs. Within a matter of seconds, every single animal in the sitting room had vanished without trace, all, that is, except for Norbert, Delilah and Colin.

"Where can *we* hide?" Delilah demanded. "Norbert and I are too big to fit anywhere!"

"Mmmmm," Colin pondered, rubbing his beak pensively. "You're quite right - it would be far easier to conceal a hippopotamus than it would to hide Norbert with that huge belly of his."

"Exactly…"

"But I'm pretty sure *you* could hide behind those long curtains over there at the back of the room."

Delilah glanced dubiously over at the curtains; whilst it wasn't the greatest of hiding places, it was certainly better than standing in the middle of the sitting room, and so off she trotted.

"But what about me, Colin?" Norbert bleated.

"I'm sorry, my dear friend, but I am afraid there is no room at the inn."

"Oh?"

"What I'm trying to say, you prize chump, is that there isn't room to hide you anywhere in the house."

"Oh?" Norbert looked around in dismay. "Where can I go then?"

"There's only one thing for it – you'll have to go outside."

"Outside? But…"

"Listen to me, Norbert. So far this evening, we have been attacked by a vampire in the barn and a witch in this very room. Based on that evidence, I would say that outside is by far your safest bet."

"Yes, but…"

"All you need to do is walk round to the back of the house and stand in the shadows. That way, nobody will see you *and* you'll be sheltered from the wind. You see? Perfect!"

"Ok, Colin. And where are you going to hide?"

"Mmm," the cuckoo peered around thoughtfully. "It would appear that all of the best hiding places are already taken down here. I think I'll try my luck upstairs…"

Chapter 11

It was a dismal and dejected Farmer Finbar that crawled back into the farmhouse that night; an evening which had begun so promisingly had once again ended in complete and utter disaster. The thing that puzzled him most of all was that he could not for the life of him understand why Mrs Muckleton had fled the premises so suddenly. *It was as if she had seen a ghost… Or had he done something to offend her?*

Closing the front door, he kicked off his big black wellington boots and went inside just as the clock in the hallway struck midnight.

"Garn," he muttered "is it that time already? Well, Finbar – I suppose you'd better be getting yourself up to bed."

It was as he was crossing the landing to the bedroom that he noticed something stuck to the carpet. Stooping to examine it, he was surprised to discover that it was a bird's feather. Moreover, it was an unusual, speckled sort of feather, and he had a vague feeling he had seen one exactly like it somewhere before, though where and when, he could not say…

*

It had not been Colin's original intention to hide in Finbar's bed. He was, after all, a highly intelligent cuckoo, and highly intelligent cuckoos do not generally hide in the beds of ferocious farmers. No, reader – his *original* plan had been to conceal himself *underneath* the bed. A brief reconnaissance of the terrain beneath the bed, however, had brought him swiftly to the conclusion that conditions there were far too hostile to sustain intelligent life for any length of time. The void beneath Finbar's bed, he now saw, was one of those dark netherworlds you read about from which none ever return, and it was this realisation that had forced him to take up his current tactical position under the duvet.

As he nestled his weary head into the pillow, Colin was aware of a strange sense of calm stealing over him. *The farmhouse stairs,* he reasoned, *were extremely creaky, and he would thus be adequately warned of Finbar's approach should the farmer return home unexpectedly.* Unfortunately, in thinking along these lines, he had failed to allow for the passage of time; whilst it was true that many years ago, when he was a young and sprightly cuckoo, he would certainly have heard the creak of the stairs as the farmer ascended, as the elderly, partially-deaf bird which he now was, he did not hear a thing.

*

Finbar was so tired that evening that he climbed into bed without even bothering to get undressed. With a customary yawn and a scratch of the ear, he closed his weary eyes and was soon fast asleep. For a short time, perhaps half-an-hour, he and Colin slumbered peacefully side by side in the bed, each blissfully unaware of the other's presence. It was, on the face of it, a happy arrangement for both parties which may well have lasted right through to the morning, were it not for Finbar's snoring.

It began as a low rumbling sort of a sound, something along the lines of a lorry climbing a steep hill; noticeable, but not loud enough to cause any kind of major disturbance. But as is often the case with snorers, the deeper the sleep into which they fall, the louder the snoring becomes; sure enough, by the time Finbar had been asleep for ten minutes, the level of decibels in the bedroom had risen to that generated by the engine of a Boeing 747 passenger jet.

"Norbert?" Colin clucked, opening his bleary eyes. "Is that you? What have I told you about sleeping underneath my tree?"

Then he remembered where he was. He was *not* tucked up safe and snug in his nest, high in the branches of the old sycamore tree; he was in Finbar's bed! And unless he was very much mistaken, Finbar was in there with him…

Hardly daring to breathe, Colin tentatively pulled back the duvet with a view to making a quick exit. Little did he know that this altogether simple action was what would prove to be his downfall. For unbeknown to the unfortunate cuckoo, Finbar had, but a moment earlier, broken wind in his sleep. Looking back at the affair in years to come, Colin would often reflect bitterly on the cruel hand that fate dealt him that night. There were so many factors which could easily have led to a different outcome. Had, for example, Finbar dined on sausages at the Halloween Party, he would have undoubtedly unleashed one of the booming salvoes for which he was renowned in the village. Had this occurred, Colin would have known that he should under no circumstances peel back the duvet and instead take some sort of appropriate evasive action. As it was, the farmer had been restricted to a mere cheeseburger, a packet of crisps and a pickled onion at the party, ingredients which had resulted only in the near-silent hiss which the cuckoo had mistaken for a leak of gas from the boiler in the attic. Thus it was that when he peeled back the cover, Colin was, without warning, hit by a wave of fumes unlike anything he had ever previously encountered in the course of his long and eventful life.

"Gug gug gug gug!" he shrieked as the noxious cloud engulfed him. This, reader, as any ornithologist will tell you, is the sound that a cuckoo makes when agitated.

Finbar, needless to say, was awake in an instant. Sitting bolt upright in his bed, he goggled in disbelief at the stricken bird as it writhed, choking and gasping on the mattress beside him Nobody, not even the most tolerant of people, enjoys waking up and finding that there is a cuckoo in their bed, and Finbar was no different.

"Garn!" he bellowed, shaking his fists with rage.

Though dizzy with the fumes, Colin recovered his senses enough to realize that he had outstayed his welcome and so, having hopped down off the bed, he skittered across to the door as fast as his spindly legs would carry him, only to discover that it was shut tight and would not budge! A roar from the other side of the room alerted him to the fact that Finbar was on the move, bearing down on him with the purposeful, plodding steps of an out-ofcondition Godzilla. The situation, as Colin saw it, left him with only two options, and for the purposes of clarity, we shall label them option A and option B. In short, they were as follows:

Option A: He could stand his ground, laughing in the face of fear, and bravely await whatever gruesome end fate had in store for him.

Option B: He could run for his life, squealing and squawking in terror, and seek refuge beneath Farmer Finbar's bed.

The cuckoo's sharp mind took less than a second to decide that Option B was the way forward, and so off he scuttled, narrowly evading the farmer's grasp.

"Garn!" Finbar roared as he saw his prey vanish beneath the bed. "Why, you pesky old bird – you come out of there this minute!"

Hunkered down in his refuge, Colin did not reply.

"Right then," the farmer snarled "if you won't come out, then I'll have to come under there and get you!" And with these chilling words, he fell to his knees and began to grovel and claw his way beneath the bedframe.

*

Out in the yard, Norbert's ears twitched; there was a terrible commotion in the farmhouse. Waddling closer to investigate, he soon discovered that the sounds were coming from an upstairs window at the rear of the building, and it was as he peered up at this window that he saw it; the unmistakeable form of a plump and rather mangy cuckoo, frantically fluttering up and down on the other side of the glass.

"Oh no," he whinnied in dismay "Colin's in trouble!"

*

"Garn!"
"Gug, gug, gug, gug!"
"Garn!"
"Gug, gug, gug, gug!"
"Garn!"
"Gug, gug, gug, gug!"
"Garn!"
"Gug, gug, gug, gug!"

Above, reader, you will find an accurate transcript of the dialogue as it occurred in Finbar's bedroom. In his assessment that his friend was in trouble, Norbert had been wholly accurate; flushed out into the open by the grasping, groping hands of the farmer, Colin had fluttered and flapped his way up onto the windowsill only to find that once again his escape route was barred, this time by a rusty old latch.

On the plus side, Finbar had, in his efforts to capture the bird, succeeded in getting his fat bottom stuck fast beneath the bedframe and was temporarily reduced to bellowing a series of curses and oaths, none of which can be reproduced here in what is, after all, a book intended for the younger reader.

Pleeeeeeese open, the cuckoo prayed as he tugged away at the latch with all his strength, but *still* it would not give. A quick glance in the direction of the bed confirmed his worst fears; Finbar had managed to free himself and was even now clambering across the bed towards him.

Sometimes, reader, things will occur for which there is no rational explanation, and these are often referred to as 'divine intervention'. *The Parting of the Red Sea* in the Bible, allowing Moses to lead the Hebrew people to freedom from the slavery of the Egyptians, is one good example of divine intervention; *the Opening of Finbar's Bedroom Window* is another.

Cornered, with no chance of escape and the terrifying hulk of Farmer Finbar bearing down on him, Colin did something he had never done before; he gave up. *His,* he reasoned, *had been a long and fruitful life, filled with joyous adventure. Ideally, he would have preferred a different ending to being beaten to a jelly by an obese farmer, but sometimes one has to take the rough with the smooth. At least he wouldn't have to put up with those long, tedious conversations with Norbert anymore...*

But it was at this very moment, just when all hope seemed lost, that the good old *divine intervention* decided to show its hand; as Colin backed, whimpering and cringing, into the corner of the windowsill, commending his soul unto God, the rusty latch inexplicably gave way, and with a faint creak, the bedroom window swung open.

"Garn!" Finbar roared. In the act of clambering over the bed, he had become somewhat entangled in the eiderdown and was horrified to see his quarry on the verge of escape. *This,* he now understood, *was the very same cuckoo that had tormented him on numerous occasions in the past, and there was no way he was going to let it get away this time...*

And so, like a puma in the jungle that has just spotted a passing antelope, he coiled his body into a pouncing position and launched himself at the terrified bird. An intelligent person would no doubt have seen the inherent dangers of launching oneself from a springy bed towards an open window; Finbar, however, was not an intelligent person. It never occurred to him for one second that the mattress might act like a sort of springboard and catapult him straight out through the open window into the cool autumn night, though this is precisely what it did. I would like to report that he soared through the night skies like an albatross on the wing, however, overweight farmers do not soar through night skies like albatrosses on the wing; they drop like stones. Or bricks – whichever you prefer…

In what initially seemed like a stroke of luck, he was saved from serious injury by a soft landing. Naturally, it came as something of a surprise to Norbert to find that a mysterious rider had suddenly landed on his back out of nowhere. More surprising still, however, was his discovery on peering over his shoulder that the mysterious rider was a ghost! In the act of leaping from the bed, Finbar had somehow managed to bring along a large white sheet which had been tangled around his midriff. During the course of the fall, this sheet had caught in the wind and wrapped itself around his head and shoulders, giving him an uncanny resemblance to the Ghost of Christmas Past.

With a whinny of fright, Norbert reared up on his hind legs in a frantic bid to dislodge the spectre.

"Garn!" it roared as it clung to the horse's mane for dear life.

This roaring, of course, only sent Norbert into an even deeper state of panic and he responded by bucking and rearing even more violently all around the yard. But *still* the ghostly rider hung on… Finally, having exhausted all other options, Norbert did what most horses would do in the circumstances; he bolted.

"Norbert!" Finbar cried as he was carried helplessly off down the lane, the sheet still wrapped around his head. "Norbert – it's me, Finbar! Stop at once, do you hear me?"

But Norbert did *not* hear him. As he trotted away into the darkness, he had only one thing on his mind; to run as far away as he could as fast as his tired old legs would carry him in the hope that the ghost would eventually leave him alone…

Epilogue

Brrrrriiiiiing!

Up at the farmhouse, Finbar woke with a start at the sound of his doorbell. Tired and groggy after his ordeal, he had barely been asleep for an hour.

"Hang on a minute," he grumbled as he hobbled down the stairs. "I'm coming!"

On opening the front door, he was surprised to be greeted by the sunny smile of Mrs Braithewaite, the lady who he had seen running the tombola stall at the Halloween party. Short, stout and radiating jolliness, she wore little round spectacles that gave her a passing resemblance to a genial owl.

"Good morning, Mr Finbar," she beamed. "Isn't it a lovely day?"

"Hmmf," the farmer grunted in reply.

"I'm so glad you're in – I've come to deliver you your prize."

"Prize?" Finbar's eyes narrowed suspiciously as they focused on a brown paper parcel that she held beneath her arm. "What do you mean, *prize?*"

"Why – the prize for best Halloween costume, silly! Mrs Muckleton handed me your entry slip when we were chatting at the tombola …"

"But…"

"All of the judges agreed unanimously that yours was the most convincing Frankenstein's monster they'd seen in years."

"Garn!"

Noticing the farmer's indignant expression, Mrs Briathewaite's face fell.

"What's wrong? Don't you want your prize?"

"Want my prize?" Finbar bellowed. "I'll tell you what you can do with your blinkin' prize, Mrs Braithewaite – you can shove where the sun don't shine!"

"Why, Mr Finbar – how very rude of you! I have never been so insulted in all my life! Well - if you are refusing to accept your prize, I'm afraid I shall have to give it to the runner up." And with this, she turned to head off down the lane.

As he watched her go, Finbar was conscious of a vague sense of triumph, until that is, his eyes once again focused on the parcel that she still clutched beneath her arm; there was something strangely alluring about the way it bulged that intrigued him.

"Mrs Braithwate," he called "wait a second!"

"Yes?" she said, stopping in her tracks.

"That there prize - what was it, just out of interest?"

"Of course, it's no longer any of your business," she replied haughtily, "but if you must know, if was a pound of sausages."

"A p...p... pound of sausages?" the farmer trembled. "Y... you don't mean..."

"Barry the butchers finest? Why – of course."

"Mrs Braithewaite," the farmer pleaded as waddled frantically down the lane to where she stood. "I... I'm sorry for being so rude. It's just that I had a bad night and..."

"I'm not interested in your excuses, Mr Finbar," she snapped. "You are a very rude man and don't deserve a prize. Now, if you are quite finished, I'll be on my way to deliver these sausages to the runner up."

Throwing himself at her feet in despair, the farmer looked up at Mrs Braithewaite imploringly.

"This... this runner up, Mrs Braithewaite..." he wept.

"Yes? What about him?"

"Is... is it anyone I know?" Even as he asked the question, Finbar was conscious of a sinking feeling in his stomach, as though he already knew in his heart of hearts what the answer would be.

"Of course it is," she replied crossly. "I saw you talking to him at the party. Old Joe Baxter's the name..."

"GAAAAAAAARN!"

*

"Norbert?" a voice clucked from high among the branches of the old sycamore tree. "Are you there?"

"Yes Colin," came the weary reply from down below.

There followed a sharp rustling of leaves as the cuckoo descended clumsily from his nest.

"I am glad you're here," he said as he alighted on a low branch "for I fear I owe you an apology…"

"Oh?"

"Yes, Norbert. When you told me you were frightened of Halloween, I mocked you. Indeed, I do believe I may even have *scoffed* at the idea."

"That's ok Colin."

"No, my dear friend – it is *not* ok. When you said you believed in vampires and witches, I laughed in your face. Yet during the course of the night we encountered those very things; a vampire in the barn and a witch in the sitting room."

"And there was a ghost…"

"Well, Norbert – that's not strictly true, is it? Have you forgotten already that the thing on your back was, in fact, Farmer Finbar draped in a white sheet?"

"Oh yes," Norbert smiled dimly. "I had forgotten that."

"Do you know you carried him for nearly twelve miles before he fell off into that ditch?"

"Oh?"

"Yes, Norbert. I didn't know you had it in you!"

"Wow!" the horse's smile quickly transformed into a look of concern. "Do you think he'll be annoyed?"

"Annoyed? A jolly old soul like Finbar – I very much doubt it…"

"Phew!"

"Anyway," the cuckoo concluded "it truly was a night of terror, and I hope to goodness we don't have the same thing again next year."

This brought a worried frown from Norbert.

"Colin?" he said. "What *will* we do next Halloween?"

"Next Halloween? Why do you ask?"

"It's just that some of the animals in the field wanted to know if you'd be staying here in your tree next year, or if you'd be spending it Farmer Finbar's bed again…"

"Let me make one thing clear," the cuckoo clucked "I did *not* spend the night in Farmer Finbar's bed, and I'd be grateful if you would refrain from going about the place spreading malicious gossip!"

"I'm sorry, Colin."

"Anyway - you can tell all of your so-called friends that I shall be spending next Halloween night in the comfort and safety of my nest."

"Oh?"

"Yes, Norbert. And if I am assailed by battalions of vampires, regiments of witches and legions of ghosts, it will be a mere picnic compared with the nameless and unspeakable horrors that abound in that terrifying *heart of darkness*, otherwise known as Farmer Finbar's bedroom..."

The End

Other titles in the "Norbert the Horse" series

Norbert

Norbert's Summer Holiday

Christmas with Norbert

Norbert to the Rescue!

Norbert – The Collection

Find out about Norbert's other adventures, horsey facts, competitions and *MORE* at

www.norbertthehorse.com

Other titles by James Sutherland

Frogarty the Witch

Roger the Frog

The Further Adventures of Roger the Frog

The Tale of the Miserous Mip

Jimmy Black and the Curse of Poseidon

Visit **www.jamessutherlandbooks.com** for more information and all the latest news!

About the Author

James Sutherland was born in Stoke-on-Trent, England, many, many, many years ago. So long ago, in fact, that he can't remember a thing about it. The son of a musician, he moved around lots as a youngster, attending schools in the Isle of Man and Spain before returning to Stoke where he lurked until the age of 18. After gaining a French degree at Bangor University, North Wales, James toiled manfully at a variety of office jobs before making a daring escape through a fire exit, hell-bent on writing silly nonsense full-time. In his spare time, James enjoys hunting for slugs in the garden, chatting with his goldfish and frolicking around the house in his tartan nightie.

Made in the USA
San Bernardino, CA
11 March 2017